Lizzie

Love
Claire
Shaw
xxx

REIGN: ROYAL BASTARDS MC

REIGN
ROYAL BASTARDS MC
MEMPHIS, TN

USA Today Bestselling Author
CLAIRE SHAW

CLAIRE SHAW

REIGN: ROYAL BASTARDS MC

REIGN - COPYRIGHT

This book is a work of fiction. The names, characters, places, and incidents are all products of the author's imagination and are not to be construed as real. Any resemblances to persons, organizations, events, or locales are entirely coincidental.

Reign. Copyright © 2023 by Claire Shaw. All rights reserved. No part of this book may be used or reproduced in any manner whatsoever without written permission from the author, except in the case of brief quotations used in articles or reviews.

For information, contact Claire Shaw.

Cover Design by Crimson Cruz

CLAIRE SHAW

REIGN: ROYAL BASTARDS MC

CONTENTS

REIGN - COPYRIGHT	III
CONTENTS	V
BLURB	VII
TRIGGER WARNING	IX
ROYAL BASTARDS MC FEATURED CHAPTERS	XI
ROYAL BASTARDS CODE	XIII
ROYAL BASTARDS MC SERIES	XV
FIFTH RUN	XV
ROYAL BASTARDS MC	XVII
MEMPHIS CHAPTER	XVII
Member List	XVII
ONE - REIGN	- 1 -
TWO - RAVEN	- 8 -
THREE - REIGN	- 16 -
FOUR - RAVEN	- 25 -
FIVE - REIGN	- 34 -
SIX - RAVEN	- 46 -
SEVEN - REIGN	- 55 -
DEDICATION	- 63 -
BOOKS BY THE AUTHOR	- 65 -
ABOUT THE AUTHOR	- 67 -
SOCIAL LINKS	- 69 -

CLAIRE SHAW

REIGN: ROYAL BASTARDS MC

BLURB

USA Today Bestselling Author Claire Shaw brings you book one in the new Memphis TN Chapter of the Royal Bastards MC

She blew back into town & my life like the tornado that she is.

Twisting and swirling my organised life, bringing chaos with her, and leaving destruction in her wake.

She was always the one that got away. My biggest regret

Now she needs me but is too stubborn to admit it

Can I let her crazy in and embrace it?

Or will it destroy us… destroy me?

CLAIRE SHAW

VIII

REIGN: ROYAL BASTARDS MC

TRIGGER WARNING

This book is intended for mature audiences only.

If darker books are not for you, please do not move forward.

After re-adjusting my trigger warning system, I will *not* be giving any spoilers.

Please understand that this is not your run-of-the-mill romance and tough subjects will be discussed in this storyline.

This story could include things like rape, kidnapping, abuse, domestic violence, drugs, alcohol abuse, and *many* other potential triggers.

CLAIRE SHAW

X

REIGN: ROYAL BASTARDS MC

ROYAL BASTARDS MC FEATURED CHAPTERS

Nikki Landis - Las Vegas, NV Chapter
Maddog, Manic and Creature

Sapphire Knight - Central Texas Chapter
Plague and Blow

Kris Anne Dean - Atlantic City, NJ Chapter
Aero and Grizzly

Chelle C Craze & Eli Abbott - Cleveland, OH Chapter
Sleeper, Sledgehammer, Ghoul, Wiley, and Crow

Morgan Jane Mitchell - Nashville TN, Chapter
Kingpin

J Lynn Lombard - Los Angeles, CA Chapter
Derange, Aftermath, Bones and Pretty Boy

Kristine Dugger - Omaha NE Chapter
The Irishman and Inferno

CLAIRE SHAW

Erin M Trejo - Savannah GA Chapter
Demon and Drake

# ROYAL BASTARDS CODE

PROTECT: The club and your brothers come before anything else, and must be protected at all costs. **CLUB** is **FAMILY**.

RESPECT: Earn it & Give it. Respect club law. Respect the patch. Respect your brothers. Disrespect a member and there will be hell to pay.

HONOR: Being patched in is an honor, not a right. Your colors are sacred, not to be left alone, and **NEVER** let them touch the ground.

OL' LADIES: Never disrespect a member's or brother's Ol' Lady. **PERIOD**.

CHURCH is **MANDATORY**.

LOYALTY: Takes precedence over all, including well-being.

HONESTY: Never **LIE**, **CHEAT**, or **STEAL** from another member or the club.

TERRITORY: You are to respect your brother's property and follow their Chapter's club rules.

TRUST: Years to earn it...seconds to lose it.

NEVER RIDE OFF: Brothers do not abandon their family.

REIGN: ROYAL BASTARDS MC

ROYAL BASTARDS MC SERIES
FIFTH RUN

Kristine Dugger: Ride it, My Pony
Lucian W Bane: Butterfly and Kult
Morgan Jane Mitchell: Royal Pain
Crimson Syn: Coerced into Submission
Claire Shaw: REIGN
Daphne Loveling: Cold Fury
Liberty Parker: Waking the Dragon
B.B. Blaque:
Kristine Allen: FACET
Erin M Trejo: Cross The Line
KL Ramsey: LEGEND
Darlene Tallman: Banshee's Lament
M Merin: THROTTLE
Chelle C. Craze & Eli Abbott: SLEEPER
Nicole James: Enforcing the Rules
Nikki Landis: Jigsaw's Blayde
J. Lynn Lombard: Aftermath's Exposure
Kris Anne Dean: No Way Out
Katie Latronico: Wherever I May Roam
India R. Adams: Praying For Lightning

CLAIRE SHAW

Kathleen Kelly: REAPER
Dani René: REBEL
Amy Davies: Kink's Redemption
Murphy Wallace: Injustice and Absolution
Jessica Ames: Out of the Storm
Jax Hart: Desert Sky
Sapphire Knight: Dirty Boy
Elle Boon: Royally Destroyed
J.A. Collard: In Too Deep
Verlene Landon: Bitten by Zombie
J.L. Leslie: Worth the Fight

Royal Bastards MC Facebook Group -
https://www.facebook.com/groups/royalbastardsmc/
Website- https://www.royalbastardsmc.com/

REIGN: ROYAL BASTARDS MC

ROYAL BASTARDS MC MEMPHIS CHAPTER MEMBER LIST

Prez - Reign
VP - Suede
SAA - Malice
Enforcer - Country
Road Captain - Tyres
Treasurer - Bench
Secretary - Mischief
Cleaner - Elvis
Tech - Cyber

Other Members - Pixel, Dixie, Firefly, Eagle

Prospect - Tracker

Club Bunnies - Rose, Daisy, and Betsy

Family Members - Banjo, Tyres Dad. Raven, Tyres sister

CLAIRE SHAW

XVIII

REIGN: ROYAL BASTARDS MC

ONE - REIGN

BEING KING is not all fun and games. Whoever said being President of an MC was all booze, pussy and living free was an uneducated idiot. I can hear my brothers in the common room, the bass from the music vibrating through the walls, dulled slightly by my closed office door.

Resting my elbows on the desk, I rub my temples, trying to get rid of the headache appearing as the numbers on the papers in front of me seem to be jumping.

Don't get me wrong, I love being President. The faith my brothers have in me is enough to vote me in, enough to blindly follow me. Okay, maybe blindly is a little strong. After all, an MC is based on respect, trust, and loyalty but also on what is best for the club as a whole. We are a family. I have my brother's backs and they have mine. We each have a role to play, not just the officers but we wouldn't be able to function as the well-oiled machine that we do without every moving part, playing its role, regardless of how small that role is.

CLAIRE SHAW

My desk looks like a paper bomb has gone off. I know I need to be more organized and sort myself out. Wonder if I can get an assistant? Do MC presidents have assistants or is it the secretary's job to help me? Yeah, I'll delegate some of this crap to the other officers.

My musing about assistants and my lack of organization is interrupted by a hammering on my door. Groaning at what someone needed now, I call them to enter. Another downside to being the President, everyone comes to you with their problems. But who do you go to with yours? This is where I guess an ol lady would be the perfect person.

I've been feeling a little disjoined with life recently. I am not getting any younger and feel like now is the time to settle down. Find my ride or die. Then again, I am pretty sure I found her years ago but as I am an asshole, I managed to lose her.

"Hey, why are you hiding?" Suede asks as his head appears around my door.

"Not hiding fucker. Going over the accounts" I grumble back

Fucker has the nerve to laugh at me, while he takes a seat on the sofa I keep in my office.

"As Treasure, isn't it Bench's job to look over the numbers?"

"He does but I also like to know what's in the accounts and how each business is doing?"

Yes, we are a one percenter club and we have less legal ways of earning green but also do have a few legal businesses. The standard garage and strip club but we also own a steakhouse, a design business which Pixel runs plus a tattoo shop and bar. The steakhouse is more upmarket and earns us a boatload but we tend not to go there much, just show our faces now and again. The Royal Grill is definitely our money maker.

"Joys of being King" Suede laughs

"Remember that next time you think you can fill this seat"

"Oh, you can keep that seat, do I fuck as like want the headache"

His head moves toward the door and slants to the side as if he's confused. I now notice the music has now stopped and all seems quiet. Too quiet and a sudden eerie feeling washes over me. Something was very wrong. Suede and I look at each other, stand and rush into the common room. All the brothers are standing around Tyres as he is freaking out.

"What is going on?" I ask no one in particular.

"Tyres got a call to say Banjo has taken a turn. Just waiting for his carer to call him back as the paramedics had just arrived." Mischief tells me.

I made my way through the brothers who had gathered around Tyres who is sat on a sofa with his head in his hands. He looks so defeated. Banjo is Tyres' dad and they are so close, he's close to all brothers here. He was never an actual member, but we made him an honorary member. Tyres also has a sister Raven. They are close siblings.

I sit next to Tyres on the sofa and place my hand on his shoulder, squeezing to show my support. His head lifts and the despair is clear as day across his face.

"We've got you brother" I promise
"I can't lose him. What will I tell Raven?"

The worry and stress on his face, makes my heart hurt for him and Raven. But also, the club as a whole. Banjo is a massive part of us. Always around when one of us needs to talk or to put us on the straight path, give us a kick in the ass when needed. Where Royal Bastards, we also need our asses kicking.

Tyres phone going off ends all quiet conversation and everyone waits withheld breaths. I can only hear Tyres side of the conversation but from what I can make out, it is not good. He nods as if the person on the end of the phone can see him and ends the call. We all look at him, waiting for news.

"Debs said they are taking him to the hospital, they think he's had a stroke. It's bad Reign. I need to reach Raven."

"I'll contact Raven, you head off to meet the ambulance at the hospital. Concentrate on your dad" Mischief tells him, getting his phone out of his pocket already.

On mass, we leave the clubhouse and follow Tres. You can see the relief and feeling of support as the club sets off to the hospital with him. It doesn't take us long to reach the hospital and park up.

The emergency room is crazy, people all over the place. They are not the most welcoming of places. No one would be here if they didn't need to be. We make it to the nurse's station, just as Tyre's name is called. Debs, who is Banjos' carer is rushing towards us.

REIGN: ROYAL BASTARDS MC

"I told them you were coming. I figured everyone would come with you so we have a private waiting room." She says as she leads back the way she came and into a private family room full of chairs but not enough chairs. We fill the available chairs and the rest of the brothers lean up against the walls or sit on the floor. Someone has tried to brighten up the room a little. It's painted a muted yellow color and artwork of flowers, landscapes and other bright-colored works hang on the walls.

In the corner on a table is a leaflet holder full of brochures giving people information on normal hospital shit like quitting smoking, weight loss and also bereavement. Hopefully, that is one brochure we won't need today.

We are not waiting long when the door opens, hoping it might be a nurse, only its Mischief.

"Sorry, I couldn't get hold of Raven. I've left her a message" he says, taking a space against the wall.

The wait seems to be forever, when waiting for news on a loved one, an hour can feel like five hours. A nurse did come in to say the doctors were still with Banjo and they were waiting for the stroke team to come and assess him. While we wait, both Tyres and Mischief keep trying to get a hold of Raven with no luck.

"Why won't she answer?" Tyres says with concern

"She might be working a case brother. You tried Sam?" Mischief asks

Raven is a bounty hunter and works alongside a giant of a man called Sam. The guy is a gentle giant. Even though he looks like he could and does eat small children for breakfast. He's a solid guy, looks out for Raven and we have no worries about him hitting on her as the dude is gay. Loves men. A certain brother has caught his eye but it's not common knowledge that this brother is open with who he's with. Greedy fuck loves cock and pussy.

Tyres tries Sam and leaves a message. Now I am a little concerned. Usually, one of them is reachable just in case something happens. Banjo's health has been an issue for a few years now but recently he has been getting worse. Tyres has mentioned that Raven was going to start to be home more rather than running state to state chasing low lives.

Finally, the doctors comes in and asks to speak with Tyres alone. They go outside and silence in the room is deafening as we all wait to find out what's happening. Looking around the room, taking in each of my brothers, you can clearly see the worry and concern on their faces. Nearly every single brother is here, including two of our club girls Betsy and Rose.

Tyres comes back not long after and is struggling to hold himself together. Debs leaps from her chair and wraps her arms around him, holding him together when he can't do it himself. We give them a moment while they embrace each other and Tyres whispers gently to her.

Debs has been great for Banjo, while only in her 30s, she took no shit from him and threw as much grumpy attitude back or ignored him when he got in one of his moods. He hates feeling like he is getting old. Tyres and Debs have become close. Definite sparks.

"It's not good. The stroke was severe and…" he takes a few moments to compose himself before carrying on. Not that he needs to, Debs is now in tears and they are holding each other up as the brothers surround them. Each lending them both their strength and support.

"He's not going to recover. Even with treatment and therapy, we are just prolonging the end. I don't want to do that to him. He would want to live like that. We need to get in touch with Raven."

Mischief nods and pulls his phone out, Cyber pulls his laptop from the bag he always has with him and starts looking for her too. We will find her; I just hope it is not too late.

CLAIRE SHAW

TWO - RAVEN

I CAN feel the sweat start to run down my back and between my breasts. The Las Vegas heat is finally getting to me. I can't run the engine so I can put the aircon on as that will draw attention to the fact that I'm sitting in my car watching the rapist prick of a skip smoke outside a run-down seedy bar on the outskirts of Vegas.

Surveillance is one of the downsides of being a bounty hunter. It is not all chasing bad guys and doing action movie stunts. This girl is no Dog The Bounty Hunter. I've been known to try to help the ones who I think are open to being helped. Those that are down on their luck and just need someone to take a minute and listen. Just for someone to understand them a little. Doesn't everyone want someone to just care about their well-being?

I watch the spineless excuse of a man finish his cigarette and go back into the bar. Clocking the black panel van parked near the alley across from the bar. I first noticed the van when I pulled into my parking spot, and recognizing the driver instantly, Manic the SAA for the Royal Bastards

REIGN: ROYAL BASTARDS MC

MC Vegas chapter. That chapter is also bounty hunters and we are clearly chasing the same skip.

The skip in question is one Tyler Cain Jeffreys lll, a trust fund reject whose family finally gave up covering for him when he raped a family friend's daughter. The said family friend happened to be a senator. A powerful senator who was out for blood. The Cain Jeffreys family, who are old money, have disowned their middle son. He is now hiding out in the seedy world that creeps around the bright lights of Las Vegas.

This is not the first time this monster has been accused of rape. During his privileged private school days and then again while away at University, each time a girl accused him of it, his family's power and money made it all go away. But this time he chose the wrong girl. Not only did Senator Hawthorne's daughter fight back, but in doing so she showed it was not consensual and managed to get his DNA under her fingernails.

Melissa Hawthorne is an amazing woman. She has shown so much strength and courage through everything. Between her father and her brother, they are not letting this go. When you also consider who her cousin is. Melissa Hawthorne is the cousin of none other than Suede. The VP of The Royal Bastards MC Memphis, the same chapter my brother is the Road Captain for. So, this is also personal for me.

Deciding I've waited long enough and Tyler should be well on his way hammered town by now, I start my truck and pull around the back of the bar. I took my Lynard Skynard t-shirt under my bra so it shows off my stomach.

CLAIRE SHAW

Taking my hair from the messy bun, I shake it out so the black raven locks fall in sexy waves, in the rear-view mirror I add a little mascara plus a red lip. Slipping my gun, Taser, and cuffs into my bag, I lock the truck and head around the front of the bar. Just as I'm entering, I give Manic a little wave.

Entering the bar, I wait a moment for my eyes to adjust to the dark, dingy, and smoked filled room. It is your typical rundown joint, wooden chairs fill the middle of the room, with booths of faded and ripped leather lining one wall. On the wall across from the booths is the bar. Dark wood with a mirrored back wall, covered in shelves filled with bottles of liquor. At the end of the bar is a corridor leading to the toilets and the back door.

It does seem that busy. Few tables are occupied and the regulars seem to be in the stools along the bar. I notice Maddog and Creature sitting in a booth, trying to blend in. Maddog is the Prez of the Royal Bastards Vegas chapter and Creature is his enforcer. They both see me but don't really show much attention to me. I know they saw me as Creature gives me a wink and a smirk crosses his face. Ignoring them, I make my way to the bar and pick an empty stool two down from the one Tyler is sitting in.

"Beer with a tequila chaser" I order when the bartender reaches me.

He goes off to get my drink and it doesn't take long before I'm shooting the shot without grimacing. Nodding for another, I take a sip of my beer.

"Pretty girl like you shooting tequila like that is as sexy as fuck" A voice says next to me. I had felt him move next to me but chose to ignore him until he spoke to me. I didn't think he would make his move this quickly.

"So only ugly girls can shoot tequila?" I ask slightly flirting back

"No ugly girls can too but fuck is it sexy when you do it" he replies licking his lips.

The act causes a shiver of revulsion to run through me but I keep the smile on the face so it doesn't show how much I hate this pathetic excuse of a man. The only way he can feel good about himself is to use his strength against those weaker than him. That doesn't make him a man, it makes him worthless in my book.

He orders more shots and I pretend to shoot them while instead using my beer bottle to hide I haven't swallowed it. I need to keep on my toes and I can't do that if I'm drunk. I act like they are affecting me. I flirt and tease him.

Moving closer and running my fingers along his arms. Pushing my breasts his way which from the way he can't seem to keep his eyes off me is definitely working. His hands are on me and it is taking everything in me not to break all his fingers.

"Let's take this somewhere, a little more private, shall we?" I say pushing myself into his body. I need to hurry this along as I can't keep pretending much longer.

"Now we are speaking the same language" he smirks as he starts to lead me round the bar and down the corridor to the back door. I see Maddog and Creature take notice and can feel them watching us.

CLAIRE SHAW

The corridor is dark and just as we make it to the door leading outside, he switches on me so fast I don't see it coming. I let my guard down by underestimating him. I thought he was a lot more intoxicated than he actually is. As the door opens, he spins me around, slamming me into the wall, causing my head to bounce off the brick with skull-splitting pain which radiates through my head. His whole-body weight is against me, forcing me back into the brick wall behind me. His hand wraps around my neck, squeezing my throat just enough to cause me pain but not completely cut off my airway.

"Think you could trick me?" he growls in my ear.

"I don't know……. What?" I stammer out, him squeezing my neck making it difficult to talk.

"Raven, I know who you are. Do you really think I wouldn't know who was coming after me? My family might have publicly disowned me but privately, I am still their son. Who knows their secrets so they will keep helping me"

This case has been fucked up from the beginning. My instinct told me he was too easy to find. The information came too quickly and just seemed on point. Normally tips we get are vague. I should have listened to my instincts.

He squeezes my neck adding more pressure until I start to see black spots across my vision. Just as I'm on the brink of blacking out, he lets up so I can gulp large breaths of air in, only for him to start all over again. I can feel my throat bruising and brings me to the edge of passing out three or four times before he stops.

"I don't understand" I try to keep playing confused.

"Of course, you don't. Women don't have the mental capacity to understand complex things. You are only good for raising children and pleasing men"

What the actual fuck. Is he deluded or what? He wouldn't be here without a woman. Ungrateful asshole. I can't stop the laugh that bursts out of me, I am done playing weak. He thinks he knows who I am, so I better introduce myself properly.

My laugh catches him by surprise but not for long as his other hand comes up, backhanding me across the face. I can feel my cheek start to swell and he must have cut me with his ring as I start to feel blood trickle down my face.

"You think you know me? You have no fucking idea who I am" I gloat to him

The anger flashes across his face and he hits me across the face again. Followed quickly with a few punches to my middle, causing me to try to bend to protect myself. Expect I don't get very far as he is still holding me by my throat. He hits me a few more times while I try every trick, I know to get away from him. He seems to know where I am going next and has a countermove at the ready. This dude is trained.

He is an evil predator who has spent time studying his prey. He knows the self-defense moves women are shown and how to get around them so he comes out on top. This is a serial rapist and abuser.

I still, as fear encompasses my body when his free hand grabs the top of my jeans, expertly flicking the button open and his hand is inside them. He is still gripping my throat, just a little harder and using his body to keep me in place.

CLAIRE SHAW

I try to move away but it is no use, his hand is now inside my underwear. I close my eyes, trying to go to a happy place as I know what is going to happen next.

Just as I feel his fingers touch where they shouldn't be touching, they are ripped away, the weight of his body is lifted from me and his hand around my throat is gone. Unable to open my eyes, I slide down the wall and curl my arms around myself. My body screams out in protest due to the damage he has caused it. I jump a little when I feel a hand on my shoulder.

"It's okay Raven. You are safe now" The voice is gentle and familiar.

Bravely I open my eyes and look up into a face which should scare me but doesn't. It has the opposite reaction, a feeling of safety envelopes me. Manic's half-skeleton tattooed face is right in front of me, as he crouches down, hands on either shoulder, I launch myself into his arms. He wraps them around me and cradles me into him.

"We got you girly, you safe now" he whispers in my ear as I cling to him like a lifeline.

The world around me starts to come back into focus and I can hear fists hitting flesh. Looking up I see Maddog standing behind Manic, watching Creature take his anger out on Tyler.

"If he is too damaged, you'll money" I warn him

"You are one tough Chica Raven," Maddog says with a small chuckle

"I try" I reply, feeling like I can be myself now.

He's right. I am tough, this will not stop me. Fuckers like him cannot be allowed to win. Oh, hell no! It might take me a little to overcome this but taking the time to process what happened here tonight does not make me weak. No one who admits they need a minute to get themselves together or need help to overcome something is weak. It takes great strength to be aware of what you need and take it.

"Let's get you back to the clubhouse and get you checked out," Manic says.

Nodding my agreement, I let Manic pick me up, cradling me softly against his large chest. I lay my head on his shoulder as we make our way to my truck.

"I'll take your truck. The others are going take fuckface into custody."

"Thank you"

THREE - REIGN

WE ARE all still waiting at the hospital. The Stroke team are running more tests on Banjo. I thank God that they seem to be doing everything they can for him. Sometimes professional people like Doctors, Police etc. look at bikers and don't bother giving it their all to help us.

They just think we are dirty, evil criminals. Not normal everyday people who just simply live our lives slightly differently to them. Have our own set rules and morals. Want to live free on the open road, with the wind on our faces and have the right to choose. We still love our mothers, well some of us who have or had amazing mothers do.

We work hard to support our families. We protect them and care for them. We definitely do not tolerate anyone including women and children being abused or mistreated. We may be gruff and a little rough around the edges but when we love someone, we love with our whole heart and soul.

REIGN: ROYAL BASTARDS MC

The club is built on trust, respect, and loyalty. We are a brotherhood, a family. I would die to protect not only my brothers but their families too. Banjo is a huge part of that. When Tyres joined the club as a prospect, he was one of the lucky ones. Lucky because his family supported his decision.

As any mother would be, Mary was a little hesitant at first. But after coming to a few family days at the club, she soon became a mother figure to the club. Even taking the club girls under her wing, making sure they were okay. She taught us that calling them whores was wrong as they enjoyed the sex as much as us so what did that make us. It was a novel approach but it worked.

We treat our club girls as part of the family, with respect. As long as they don't cause any issues. Thank god the girls we have at the moment are amazing. I could even see a brother or so taking them as ol ladies. Unheard of I know but again as I said, our club girls are a little different. They get paid to keep the clubhouse, cook etc. but they don't have to sleep with the brothers. They have every right to say no.

It was a sad day in the club when Mary died.

Mary and Banjo had children a little later in life, after trying for years they had all but given up when Tyres came along, and then a few years later the miracle of Raven. Mary had poor health from being a child but it didn't stop her from living life to the full.

Her death was still a shock. We had all been enjoying a family Sunday and Mary said she was starting with one of her headaches that she sometimes got. Banjo took her home and that was the last time we saw her. She died that night of a brain aneurysm. At least her passing was quick and painless. Not so painless for her family or the club.

We mourned her as a club but also with Tyres, Raven, and Banjo as family. Supporting each other, which is what we will do again. All rally around Tyres and Raven, when we find her.

A nurse coming in brings me out of musings.

"Mr. Hilton has been taken to a private room. I can take you up there now, we have another waiting room for you on that floor. We advise two at a time to sit with him" she says.

We all get up and follow her through the hospital, up to a ward. The waiting room she shows us looks pretty much the same as the last one but this one is pale blue. The artwork looks the same. The chairs however look a hell of a lot more comfy than the previous ones. Thank fuck as my back is killing me.

Why do hospitals do that? They know people are going to be sitting on the chairs for sometimes hours, so make them the most uncomfortable pieces of shit known to man. Plastic, hard and not big enough for a large man like me and my brothers. These chairs are a little larger and have padding.

"Mr. Hilton is in room three zero five, which is just across the hall. Please remember only two at a time" she says before leaving us.

Tyres goes first with Debs, while the rest of us wait our turns to see him.

"Have you reached Raven yet?" I ask Mischief, as he's sat playing with his phone.

"Not yet Prez. I'll keep trying. Going to step out and try Sam again."

Nodding he leaves the room, phone already to his ear. Everyone is quietly waiting, not having much to really talk about. The girls are huddled in a corner together, I can see Elvis keeps looking over at Rose. The pair have been making eyes at each other for a long time.

They think no one else notices the looks that pass between them. Also, the little touches and moments. I wish they would just fuck it out of their systems or make a go of it. Rose is one of the best club girls we have. Her cooking is amazing. Plus, she doesn't cause issues like I know chapters and other clubs have had with their club girls.

I'll leave them be for now but depending on how long they let this go on for, I might need to step in. Have a little word in their ear and push them in the right direction. No one will think less of them for being together. That is not how this club works and they fucking well know it.

Debs comes back and asks if I would like to go next. The poor girl looks worn out and stressed. Getting out of my chair, I pull her into my arms and give her a big hug. She cuddles into me, taking some of the strength I am giving her. Banjo means a lot to her. Debs has no family as she grew up in foster care. Banjo became her family. They were more than employer and employee. She would have cared for him for free if she could have.

I pass Debs off to Country as he steps up to take over the hug. I know the girls will look after her. Leaving the waiting room, I wait a few minutes outside Banjo's room. Gearing myself up for what might greet me. Taking a deep breath, I knock lightly and enter. No amount of time could have prepared me for the sight in front of me.

Banjo is lying absolutely still in a hospital bed, with wires and tubes coming from him, hooked up to a machine keeping him alive. He looks pale and so small lying there. Not the larger-than-life man full of joy we are used to. It takes me a few minutes to be able to move from my spot near the door and walk around to the chair on the other side of his bed.

I quietly sat down and carefully took Banjo's hand in mine and gave it a soft squeeze. Just enough to let him know I was here. Nothing was said for a few minutes. Tyres and me just soaking up what had transpired in the last 24 hours.

"Anyone get a hold of Raven?" Tyres asks quietly

"Mischief is still trying and he's going to keep trying Sam too. Don't worry, we'll get in touch with her" I promise

"Feels wrong" he mutters

"Of course, it does, no one wants to see their parent like this brother" I try to reassure him

"No, I mean Raven. She has never not been reachable like this. Yeah, I've rung her before and she's not been able to answer but she has always called back. Never. Not once has she ever not been reachable for this length of time." The worry in his voice is clear to hear.

"Concentrate on your dad brother, leave finding Raven to us. I understand your feelings and don't discount them.

We should always trust our guts and instincts. If yours are telling you that something ain't right then I'll take that to the bank, as you have never steered me wrong before."

"Thanks, Prez"

We sit for a little longer in silence. Both of us lost in our own heads. I know what he means about Raven. That girl has always had a way of creeping into my soul. Raven is a few years younger than me and used to come around the club when Tyres was prospecting. I had not long patched in and was still a little green behind the ears.

The first time I saw her, it was like she cast a spell on me. I yearned to be near her, talk to her and just be in the same space as her. I didn't understand the feelings then plus she was too young. We became friends and I kept my feelings from her. Then it was too late, she was off to college and then trained in her current job as a bounty hunter. We made sure she has extra training but it kills me to watch her leave and not be mine.

"Nurses said we can talk to him and he might be able to hear us," Tyres says

"You think?"

"Who knows, worth trying I guess?"

"What would we say?"

"Fucked if I know. Anything I guess" he shrugs

Anything, okay I can do this. I can think of something to say to him. Maybe a memory or a funny story. I guess anything will do, especially if he can't hear me anyway.

"Hey, old man. If you wanted attention, I am sure there this an easier way than this" I say

Tyres chuckles at my words. What the fuck else am I going to say. I figured go with funny.

"You know we would have come with one telephone call. Fuck Dad, this is so dramatic. Shit a chick would pull" Tyres joins in

"Could have come to the clubhouse, don't need an invite. Never needed one before when your old ass would show up to check we were behaving."

"Oh fuck, remember the time he showed up as I didn't answer the phone and caught me with a girl. Jesus, talk about being caught with ya pants down. I had my dick in her and he strolls in and says "When finished son I'll be at the bar. Don't forget to be a gentleman and let the lady come first"

We both fall around laughing. When Tyres came rushing downstairs after Banjo as he swaggered back into the common room. We couldn't believe he had said that. Poor Angela was mortified as Banjo knew her dad. She never did come back to the clubhouse to party again.

"Fuck they were good times. He was a steady support for me when I got voted in as Prez. I didn't think I could handle it at first but Banjo made me realize I was made for the role and could handle anything thrown at me as I had the support of my brothers. Told me to lean on my offices and listen to everyone's points of view. Best advice I ever got."

"Sometimes It was like living with Dr Phil or Jerry Springer when Raven and I got going as kids. He broke up many arguments and made us see the other side of it. He was a good parent, couldn't have asked for better."

Standing, I place my hand on his shoulder and squeeze.

"I'm going to see if Mischief has had any luck. I'll give you a few minutes before any brother comes in. Everyone is still here and would like to see him."

He gives me a nod as he composes himself and I leave him to it. No one can blame him for being emotional at a time like this. We are men, not robots.

I make it back to the waiting room and tell Suede to go next. Mischief is back and sitting in the corner on his phone still so I go join him.

"Any news?" I ask

"Yeah, but not sure you or Tyres are going to like it." Well fuck!

"Spit it out then, can't do anything unless I know what the fuck is going on" I demand

"I managed to get a hold of Sam. He was in a car accident and is currently laid up with a broken leg. Raven said she had an easy skip and went on her own to Vegas for him. Since I called him, Sam looked into this easy skip a little more."

I feel I am not going to like the next words out of my brother's mouth. Why did she go on her own?

"The skip she went after is that fucking rapist prick Tyler Cain Jeffreys."

Yeah, I knew I would like it. My blood feels like ice in my veins at that sick fuckers name. Prick is pure fucking evil.

"Sam dug a little more and said our Vegas chapter was also hunting him. So, it might be worth reaching out to Maddog and asking if they have seen Raven."

It's a good idea, I pull my phone from inside my cut and step outside to make the call I am dreading.

"Hello" he answers after a few rings

"Maddog, Its Reign from Memphis"

"Now then brother, how's life?"

"Not so good. I am hoping you can help me?"

"If I can you know we will," something in his voice tells me he knows why I might be calling

"We are trying to reach Tyre's sister Raven. She's a bounty hunter who we think might be in your area chasing a skip. Can you see if anyone has seen her or keep an eye out? It is life or death we reach her"

"Life or Death?"

"Her dad has been taken ill; it is not good Maddog. She needs to be here to say goodbye"

"Fuck, okay I will pass the message on"

"You know where she is?" Fuck!

"Prez to Prez. Yeah, I know where she is but have been asked not to say. I will pass the urgent message on but brother, I will not break her confidence."

"I can understand that. I don't like it but I understand it. I appreciate you passing the message along"

"Talk soon"

The line drops and I know whatever is happening I am going to lose my shit over it. I can feel it in my bones. Shit will be coming at us from both sides.

REIGN: ROYAL BASTARDS MC

FOUR - RAVEN

THE DOC has patched me up and told me to rest. Maddog has let me stay in a room at the clubhouse and has promised not to tell anyone I am here. No, he wasn't happy about it. We came to the compromise that if anyone asked, he would say he knew where I was and would pass a message on but wouldn't give details. I could live with that.

My injuries are not as bad as I first thought. The ones on the outside anyway. My neck is bruised and sore. Talking and swallowing hurts but the ice chips Manic got me are working a treat. My ribs are bruised but nothing is broken, same for my face.

I am battered and bruised but whole. Inside is a different matter. No, technically he didn't rape me but he touched me in a private place without my consent. That to me is still rape. I did not give him permission to put his hand or fingers anywhere near my pussy. He took that from me.

I've had several showers now, trying to wash the feel of his hands on my skin. My breasts have finger marks on them so I keep myself covered up, then I don't have to look at them. I tried to sleep earlier but woke from a nightmare of reliving it again. Manic heard me and came to check on me.

He was so sweet and offered to stay with me so I felt safe. I won't tell anyone how sweet he is as I don't want to ruin his badass image or street creed. But I did feel safer knowing he was in the room with me and managed to sleep.

It's been a whole 24 hours since it happened and I am starting to feel a little better about it. I can't hide here forever. Tyler is in custody and can't hurt anyone anymore. I need to learn the valuable lessons this has taught me. Once I am home, I need to get back in the gym and brush up on my fighting skills.

More self-defense classes and training harder. Women shouldn't need to train like this but it is now a fact of life while low-life scum such as Tyler think they own women and can take whatever they want, just because they are men and have money.

A knock on the door comes and I call out for whoever to come in.

Maddog comes in and finds me curled up in the middle of the bed, flicking through the channels on the TV.

"You, okay?" He asks, perching himself on the side of the bed.

"I'm getting there," I answer honestly

"Glad to hear it girly. You know if you need anything, ask?"

"I do. Thank you Maddog" I give him my best smile and it seems to relax him a little.

"Have you checked in at home at all?"

"No. I've not even switched my phone on. I needed a minute to myself"

"That I can understand. I am sorry to be the one that bursts the bubble. Girly, you need to contact home." I can see his body tense up again, causing me to panic a little.

"Something wrong?" I ask as I reach for my phone sitting on the bedside table.

"Girly, your brother, and his chapter have been trying to reach you. Your daddy is in the hospital"

I freeze, phone midway to me. Fear once again coats me; this time is a different type of fear. A gut-wrenching, bone-deep fear.

"My daddy is where?" I ask in a whisper

"Call your brother. I will sort you out a flight as quickly as possible." He pats my hand like I'm a scared animal, which at this moment I probably look like one, and leaves me to call my brother.

With shaking hands, I switch my phone and the minute it powers up, the thing starts going crazy. Notification after notification comes through. Missed calls from my brother, Debs, Mischief and even Reign. Text messages from them and Sam also come through. Trust Sam to text, he hates calling people and talking on the phone. Once they finish coming through, I take a deep breath and call my brother.

"Raven" he shouts down the phone

"Jonas" I can hear the stress and panic in his voice

"Fuck you had me scared Raven."

"I am so sorry."

"I know, I've got you now. Raven, you need to come home, as quickly as possible."

"Jonas, what is going on?"

"I really didn't want to tell you over the phone but Raven, Dad had a stroke"

The minute the words leave his mouth my world crumbles. A sob escapes before I can stop it. I can hear Jonas calling my name but I can't answer him. I feel a hand on my back as another takes the phone from my grasp. I can hear more talking but I am too far gone to take in what is being said. Manic is now in front of me, pulling me once again into his arms.

"Maddog got you on a last-minute flight back to Memphis in a few hours. You still have time to make it to say goodbye Raven. Hold onto that while you get there." he tells me

I take his words in. I need to be strong now. Taking some deep breaths, I compose myself and start to make plans. This will help me stay strong if I have things to keep me busy.

"Come on, let's get you sorted and I will drive you to their airport. Tyres said he would have someone meet you at the other end to drive you straight to the hospital."

Nodding, I head to the bathroom and wash my face, trying to reduce my now puffy eyes from crying. Giving up the job as it's not working, I dry my face and rummage through my bag for makeup. Finding my foundation, I apply it as expertly as possible to cover the bruising. Not my first-time hiding bruising from the men in my life.

REIGN: ROYAL BASTARDS MC

As a bounty hunter, you tend to get knocked about a little so after the first few times of coming home with bruises, my dad and Jonas losing their shit, I learnt to hide them. I check myself in the mirror and don't think I have done too bad of a job. Gathering the rest of my things, I pack my bag and dress for the flight.

My mind is running at a million miles a second. I cannot focus on what I am going home to. I need to focus on just getting home and seeing my dad. My dad is everything to me. We have such a close bond. I really am a daddy's girl for sure. After Mom died, Dad and Jonas are all I have left.

The club stepped up more when Mom died, helping us all through the tough period of losing the heart of our family. I know my mom meant a lot to the club too. A few of the brothers either no longer have moms or had shitty moms growing up. My mom kind of adopted them as her own. Mothering them when they needed it the most.

It is the same with dad. He took on the role of older male influence for them. Being the guide when they needed it the most and also teaching them what their own fathers should have taught them about being upstanding men, how to treat women, care for them, and protect them.

Reign being the one who soaked that up like a sponge. Reign and my dad are close too. Which made it more difficult when I developed a teenage crush on him. He never shared the same feelings back. We were friends and I was okay with that. I knew what I wanted to do in life, college and then bounty hunter was the end goal.

In my heart, I knew I need to grow up and have those life experiences before I could settle down, and build a life with someone. Manic pops his head around the bedroom door, asking if I'm ready to go. With a deep breath, a grab my bags and head out. As we walk through the common room all the brothers give me a hug and tell me I got this. I feel the strength they are trying to give me, seeping into my soul, and building me up.

It doesn't take long to get to the airport and get checked in for my flight. I hate waiting around with nothing to do but thankfully it doesn't take too long and I am boarding the three and a bit hours flight home. I use the time in the air to center myself and get control of my emotions.

Jonas is going to need me to be strong for him. He never has been very good with emotions, typical badass man. But as we get older and the influence of the club, he's got a lot better. This is down to the brothers showing him men can have emotions and it is normal to show them.

Thank God the flight seems quick and before too long, we have landed. I hate flying. I don't mind the middle part as I usually have my Kindle with me so I can read. It is the taking off, landing and any turbulence which gets to me. Turbulence seriously freaks me out.

I exit the plane and make my way through arrivals, missing luggage out as I only had carry-ons, making it outside I look for my ride. It doesn't take long for me to spot one of my favorite people standing next to a club SUV. I take off running, dropping my bags next to him as I leap into Mischief's open arms.

"Fuck Raven, am I glad to see you," he tells me as he holds me tight. I try not to show any pain as he holds me a little too tight for my battered body.

"I know and I am sorry," I tell him as I slide down his body and pick my bags up from next to us.

Mischief takes them from me, putting them on the back seat before opening my door. Ever the gentleman, he helps me inside which works in my favor since I could use the help until I'm healed but I can't really tell him that. He is already looking at me with his head tilted as he is trying to work it out.

"You look different. Are you wearing more makeup than usual?" he asks

Fuck, shit, wank. I was really hoping no one would notice I had on more makeup than usual. My previous bruises were only light but these ones are not so it took a little more than before to cover them. Clearly, this is going to be very noticeable as normally I hardly wear makeup except for a little mascara and lipstick.

"No, nothing more than usual. I was a little puffy from having a little cry so I put a little extra on, don't want Jonas worrying"

I pray to God he doesn't push further. I hate lying but this is their own good and mine. They will all be under enough stress with what's happening with Dad, they really don't need me adding to it.

He nods and closes the door. Thank fuck. He climbs in and we head off to the hospital. The closer we get the more nervous I feel. My leg is bouncing and I can't seem to stop it. Mischief moved his hand to rest on my knee too quickly, making me flinch. I can see out of the corner of my eye; he noticed and is now looking at me with wariness and concern.

"It is going to be okay; we are all here for you" he tries to reassure me.

I nodded, not trusting myself with words and squeezed his hand on my knee. We spend the rest of the drive to the hospital in silence while his hand rests comforting on my knee. Occasionally giving it a slight squeeze of reassurance. Parking up at the hospital, I take a deep lung filling breath before exhaling all my anxiety.

I follow Mischief through the hospital and to the floor my dad is on. Stopping outside the room, Mischief folds me into his arms and holds me tight.

"Club is in the waiting room opposite. This is your father's room; you want to go in or do you want me to get Tyres to come out first" he asks

God, do I love this man. Always thinking about others. For a rough and gruff biker, he has such a gentle soul.

"I think I'd like to see Tyres first please?"

He kisses my head and lets me go. I lower myself into a chair outside the room and my head sinks into my hands. I have no idea what I will be walking into. My dad has always been this larger-than-life character, so strong. I feel someone crouch in front of me, taking my hands in theirs. Instantly I know it's my brother. I fold myself into his embrace.

"I got you now sis, all is going to be okay" he whispers while stroking my hair

"I am so sorry I wasn't here when you both needed me," I sob.

"You are here now, that's the main thing. Are you ready to go see him?"

I shake my head, suddenly feeling like a small child again. I need my big brother to support me.

"We got this. Together."

We stand up and with a few deep breaths, we enter my dad's hospital room, hand in hand.

FIVE - REIGN

I AM sitting at Banjo's bedside when Mischief sticks his head in the room to say Raven is outside. Tyres gets up and goes outside to her. Mischief joins me with Banjo giving the siblings some time together. I can tell from the expression on his face and his body language, he has something to say.

"I'm telling you this as I am aware of your feelings for Raven and I don't want to pile more shit onto Tyres already burdened shoulders. There is something very wrong with Rave."

This instantly has me on alert for two reasons. One, he knows about my feelings for Raven. I didn't think anyone knew and I sure as fuck did not tell anyone. Two, what fuck does he mean something is wrong with Raven? I'm on my feet in seconds.

"Explain, now!" I growl out

"Calm Prez. She is going to need you to be calm."

On his warning, I let my now stiff body relax and lower myself back into my seat. To ground myself further for whatever he is about to tell me, I hold Banjo's hand.

"I picked her up from the airport and noticed she was wearing more shit than usual on her face. Asked her about it and she fed me bullshit about hitting puffy eyes from crying. Considering the shit on her face is covering more than just under her eyes, I call bullshit. On the drive over she was nervous which is understandable but when I reached out to comfort her, she flinched. Fucking flinched like she thought I was going to hit her."

The anger and rage vibrates through my entire being. Someone hurt her. My girl.

Fuck I have not thought of her as my girl in years but that is what the sexy hurricane that is Raven is for me. I soak up the information he's given me and form a plan in my mind.

"Okay, let's keep an eye on her. You are right, we won't burden Tyres with this while they are dealing with Banjo's health. We can't keep this from him. It is his sister."

With that said, the door opens and Tyres enters the room, hand in hand with Raven. The second I lay eyes on her, my heart stutters in my chest. It has been a few years since I last saw but fuck, she has gotten more beautiful. I can now see what Mischief means. It's clear she is covering bruises up, no matter how good of a job she's done trying to hide them.

As I take more of her face in, I notice a cut on the top of her cheek and when our eyes meet, hers takes my breath away and not in a good way. Fear, pain and also strength meet me. Someone has hurt her and I'm going to find out who. When I do, I am going to make them pay greatly for causing her this.

"We will give you some privacy," I say, giving Banjo's hand a final squeeze and then leaving the room. Not before stopping in front of Raven and placing a kiss on her forehead. No words are exchanged.

I join the rest of the club in the waiting room. Over the last 24 hours or so, we have each taken it in turns to sit with Banjo and say our goodbyes. He's holding on but the decision was made once we had Raven here and she said her goodbyes, they would stop treatment and let him pass in pace with dignity. Every person deserves that.

We all sit, lost in our own memories of Banjo. No one wants to say anything out loud. Guess that would make all this real then. Not that we think he is suddenly going to jump out of bed and be better. But talking like he's gone, makes him actually gone.

It is a few hours later that Tyres comes into the room. He doesn't need to say a word, it's on his face.

"He's gone" his voice showing his emotions.

He walks straight over to Debs who is sobbing in the corner, picks her up and sits down in the chair with her curled in his lap. Burying his face in her hair as they hold each other. I nod to Mischief and slip out the door.

I find Raven in the room with Dad. She is still holding his hand but her face is dry. Her eyes never move from his face. He looks peaceful as if he's asleep. I sit in the chair next to Raven who doesn't acknowledge my presence.

Vacant eyes remain on her dad. I take her other hand in mine, so she at least knows she's not alone.

"He's gone?" It sounds like a question, but it is more of a fact.

"Yeah, sweet girl, he's at peace now" not really knowing what to say to make this easier for her.

"Do you think he's with Mom now?"

I smile at the fact she thinks of this. The relationship her folks had, the love and a strong bond are what we all crave in our lives. Everyone, even outlaw bikers deserve to be loved.

"Definitely, a love like they had. No way they wouldn't find each other in heaven"

This idea that they are together seems to calm her. Not totally at peace with her dad's passing but is able to find something in that sadness to see the light again. The hope he has now been reunited with the love of his life.

"Not sure I can leave him all alone Reign" she admits in a whisper.

"He won't be alone, precious. A couple of brothers will stay with him and he will get an escort to the funeral home. He might not have been a patched member but he was part of the club. He will get a full biker funeral."

"He would get a kick out of that. Loved the sight of you all riding together in formation," she says with a smile.

"Come on Precious, let's get you home. After that long flight, you'll be wanting to get clean and sleep" I say as I guide her out of the seat.

"I don't want to be alone, Reign" she whispers, breaking my heart with just a few words.

"You never have to be alone. We can stop at your place and grab some things then you can stay at the clubhouse" I promise kissing her head.

"I would like that, thank you," her voice sounds so small

Leaning over she kisses her dad's head before pressing her forehead to his.

"I love you Daddy" she whispers, causing me to look away to hide the emotion swirling around in me. I promise at that moment to protect her at all costs.

Wrapping my arm around her I guided her from the room. Country and Eagle were standing guard on either side of the door. Both gave Raven big hugs.

"We will stay with him now Raven." Country says in that cowboy twang of his.

"Thank you, Country and you Eagle,"

"Your dad meant a lot to us. This is our way of honoring him" Eagle assures her.

Nodding my thanks to them both, I move us into the waiting room to join everyone else. The minute we are in the room, Raven is pulled from my grasp and passed around so everyone can show their love and support. Even when she and Debs are hugging each other, she still doesn't cry. Just stares at me like she can see into my soul. I leave her to the girls and find Tyres.

"I am taking Raven to get some stuff from her place and then going back to the clubhouse. She's agreed to stay for a while."

"Thanks, Prez, I will feel better knowing she is close"

I give him a man hug and go to retrieve Raven from the girls. We head out to the parking lot and I'm glad I had the prospect bring the club's SUV to the hospital. Suede will make sure my bike gets back to the clubhouse. I opened her door and help her inside.

On the drive to her house which is not too far from the clubhouse, I leave her to her thoughts. If she wants to talk, that's fine but I won't push her. We need to take this at her pace. As long as she knows I am here for her but also all the brothers and club girls are too.

I pull into her drive and park. Both of us just stare up at the house, not attempting to make a move.

"I'll run in and grab some stuff," she says finally getting out of the SUV and going into the house.

I pull my phone out and send a few messages. Asking the girls to get the room next to mine ready for Raven and also a room next to Tyres for Debs as I know she'll not want to be on her own either. I sent another message to Tracker to check the kitchen and do a grocery run. The passenger door opening makes me jump. I hear her tinkle of a giggle.

"Make you jump?" she asks still giggling at me

"Maybe" I grumble, making her giggle again, the sound hitting me right in the gut. I never want to miss that sound again.

She gets back into the SUV and we set off to the clubhouse. I switch the radio on for a little background music and tuned it to the local country music station. Raven started singing along to, "Thought you should know" by Morgan Wallen. Her beautiful voice flowed through the car. She looks angelic, hands out the open window as her hair blows in the breeze.

The drive is over too quickly and we back down the earth with a bump. Parking the SUV, she glazes up at the clubhouse.

"I miss him already" she admits

"That is normal precious"

She doesn't reply, we leave the SUV and I grab her bags from the back. Hand on the bottom of her lower back, I guide her into the clubhouse and up to the room she'll be staying in. I know it is not much, just a king-size bed, bedside tables, a dresser with a TV, a comfy couch, and a small table with chairs. At least this room has an en-suite.

"I know it isn't much, but it's clean and comfy. Plus, I am just next door if you need anything" Suddenly feeling nervous.

"This is perfect, thank you Reign"

"You are welcome. I'll leave you to get settled in" I say as I drop her bags at the bottom of the bed.

Closing the door, I leave her to it. I head for my office to start making arrangements for the funeral. Not sure how long I have been sitting in my office, making calls when a knock sounds at my door. It is a rule around here that if my office door is closed then you knock and wait. Otherwise, my door is usually open. I shout they can enter.

Suede, Tyres, and Mischief all come in. Suede sits in his normal spot on the couch I keep in here and Mischief joins him. Tyres takes a seat in one of the chairs in front of my desk. He looks exhausted.

"You okay brother?" I ask him

"As good as can be expected, I guess. How's Raven?" he asks

"I put her in the room next to mine and left her a few hours ago to get sorted. Figured she would need sleep after travelling and being at the hospital. I put Debs in the room next to yours" I tell him.

"Thanks, Prez, Debs came back with the girls. I wanted to stay and escort Dad."

"I can understand that. I have started the arrangements for you, less you need to organize the better"

"Again, thank you, Prez. I have no idea where to start with a funeral so the help is greatly appreciated. Something tells me I am going to need to focus elsewhere"

"Raven will be fine; we will all be here for her brother," Suede says from his relaxed position on the couch.

"Thanks, VP, but that's not what I meant. I noticed the crap on her face covering bruises and also the cut. Thinks she's been fooling us all these years covering up any bruises she got while on a skip but we knew. Just decided not to mention it to her. I also noticed the kiss and attention you have been showing her Prez."

I meet his stare, not backing down. Now is not the time to show weakness. My gut is telling me this is right. Raven is mine.

"I'll be honest. Had feelings for Raven for a long time but knew the timing wasn't right for us. First, she was too young, then I knew she wanted to go out into the world and experience life. Never want to hold her back or step on her dreams. But now she needs me, not just to help with her grief but also because I saw the bruising, the cut, and the fear in her eyes. I'll take it her pace and be respectful but I am letting you know now, Raven is mine"

I let that soak in, not sure how he is going to react but I gave him my word. I will respect her needs and go at her pace. I've waited this long for her; I will wait longer if I need to.

"I knew you had feelings for her before. You thought you hide it well, but you didn't." he laughs

"Dad knew too. He said when the time was right, he would give you, his permission. We both knew you would do right by her. Not sure if you are aware or if I should be telling you this at all but Raven had a crush on you too back then and I think she might still have feelings for you too. But Prez, don't hurt her."

"I promise, I won't do anything to hurt her. Let me deal with the funeral for you. Banjo wasn't a patched member but he was still a part of this club so will be getting a full Royal Bastards funeral. Other chapters will be coming to pay their respects. You focus on Raven and whatever happened in Vegas as we know something did"

"On it Prez"

All three leave my office and I get back to arranging the funeral, which is set for in a few days' time. After a call to Jameson from the mother chapter, he sends his condolences and said he would be sending Powertrain for the funeral. Getting a headache from talking to too many people and noticing it is now late, but I have managed to arrange the funeral. It is definitely time for bed.

A few days later and the funeral is today. The clubhouse is a hive of activity. The club girls have arranged the clubhouse for room for visitors to sleep and to make life easier we have arranged for the wake to be catered.

Raven hasn't really dealt with anything. Since coming to the clubhouse, I have not seen her smile once. She is like a zombie, just going through the motions. Her being in the room next to mine is a blessing and a curse. I like having her close but it also means I can hear her crying out in her sleep.

Nearly every night now I have ended up in her room, holding her tight so she can sleep. I make sure I am gone before she wakes up so nothing is awkward. This being gentleman fucking sucks. I want her so bad, my body aches for her. But she's not ready so I will remain her rock until she is.

I am in the common dressing in a black button-down shirt, new black jeans, my good boots, and my cut which has had a clean special for today. The brothers are dressed similarly but in dark-colored button-down shirts. Tyres is here but I don't see Raven. I head back to her room to check on her. I find her sitting on the edge of her bed in tight black jeans and a lace black shirt. She looks sad but beautiful.

"Are you ready, precious?" I ask her.

"Don't think I can do this Reign," the sadness in her eyes breaks a piece of me.

"It is never easy saying goodbye precious but you will regret not going. You can ride behind me and I will be at your side through the whole service" I promise her

"Promise you won't leave me?"

"I promise, swear it on my cut," I say as I pull her up and into my arms. Placing a soft kiss on her forehead.

"I got you precious"

"I know, thank you. You have been my rock the last few days."

I want to puff out my chest and peacock strut at her words. I want her to lean on me and know I have her back.

"Don't think I don't know you have been slipping to bed with me when I need your strength. Thank you for not making a big deal out of it. I feel safe when you are with me" she admits

"Anytime you need me, I am there for you"

I walk with Raven back down to the common room and meet everyone else, we all head outside and to our bikes. I straddle my baby and fire her up, holding my hand out for Raven. She places her small hand in mine and gets on behind me. Wrapping her arms around me and snuggling into my back. A wave of rightness crashes over me. This is where she is meant to be, on the back of my bike and in my life as my ol lady.

I pull forward and wait at the open gates for everyone else to get into position behind me. The hearse is waiting so as it starts to pull away, I raise my arm and signal to move out. We move as one, in formation and follow the hearse all the way to the graveyard. As we get closer, biker line the way with members from our other chapters all there to pay their respects.

We park up and I help Raven off. I can feel the shake in hand as I wrap my arm around her and follow the coffin. The graveyard is packed. I spot stood among the mourners,

Powertrain from the mother chapter with Plague and Blow from Central Texas.

Aero and Grizzly have also made it from Atlantic City, along with Sleeper, Sledgehammer, Ghoul, Wiley, and Crow from Cleveland. Kingpin is also here from our Nashville chapter.

I give them all the standard chin lifts as my brothers fill the chairs left empty for us. Tyres sits first with Debs beside him and then Raven with me still holding her hand. The brothers and club girls fill the remaining chairs. Throughout the service, which for a funeral wasn't as bad as some I keep a hold of Raven's hands, never letting go.

I scan the faces in the crowd and give a nod to Derange, Aftermath, Bones and Pretty Boy from our Los Angeles chapter, not far from them is The Irishman and Inferno from Omaha with Demon and Drake from Savannah.

It shows how much each of the chapters thought of Banjo and that some have travelled so far just to show their respects to his family and the club as a whole. It's a proud feeling to be part of Royal Bastards MC.

The funeral is over quickly and we make our way back to the clubhouse for the wake. Raven takes off for her room as soon as we are back. She really is struggling with everything.

SIX - RAVEN

I AM not sure how I have held it together through the funeral or the last few days. If it wasn't for Reign I would have buckled under the weight of the pain in my chest. The pain of missing my dad and knowing I am never going to see him again is consuming me.

The guilt of taking too long to get here, of not being home in the first place. The weight of the decision I made to go after Tyler on my own, the consequence of that decision and the knock-on effect that has had. I'm not sleeping properly, hardly eating, and just cannot seem to find my way out of the fog.

After the funeral, I don't hang around for the wake. Just head straight to my room, closing the door on the outside world. I quickly strip my clothes off and throw them into the laundry basket. In the bathroom, I turn the shower on as hot as it will go and step under the spray.

The heat burns my skin but I revel in it. I grab my loofa and apply a generous amount of shower gel, then scrub every inch of my skin, trying to get clean again. Once I've scrubbed so hard my skin is red raw, I collapse into the bottom of the shower, wrap my arms around my legs and sob. Huge giant unstoppable sobs break loose, skittering from the gaping wound in my chest.

I don't how long I stay curled up in the shower but just as the water turns cold, the curtain is torn back and the water is switched off. I can hear someone cursing and then a warm fluffy towel is wrapped around me as I become airborne only to land in strong arms.

"It's okay precious, I got you" I recognize Reign's voice.

I felt him dry me quickly and then something soft was placed over my head, covering me. Reign moved me to the bed, gently placing me down after folding the sheets back. He climbs in behind me and carefully starts to brush my hair. The intimate feeling of him taking care of me warmed my heart. Once he was finished, he curled his large body around mine.

"Sleep Raven." and that is exactly what I did, safe in his arms.

I wake to the feeling of something heavy around my waist. Panicking, I look down and notice the tattoo on the arm which instantly calms me. Reign. His large body is curled protectively around me. The feeling of safety envelops me.

"Morning" a gravelly morning voice sounds from behind me.

"Morning"

"You sleep, okay?"

"I did, thank you. Did you?"

"Slept like a baby with you in my arms" he admits, making my heart beat a little faster.

"Need to talk about it" he warns

"It's grief. I'll work through" I promise

"Not just grief, Precious. See the bruises and marks, see the fear in your eyes. Fuck that fear guts me. Never want to see fear like that on your face"

I thought I was doing a good job of hiding my injuries, of making sure no one saw anything different other than a grieving daughter. I was hoping, wishing, no one would need to know what happened in Vegas. Pipe dreams clearly. I need to put my big girl pants on and face the music.

I move out of his grasp and he lets me, knowing I need space to tell this story. I gather my strength and sit crossed-legged on the other side of the bed. Leaving some space between us.

"This is at your pace. You can give me just facts or full details, you need to stop, then we stop" fuck this man is breaking down all my walls.

"I was in Vegas on a skip. Decided to go it alone as Sam was in a car accident from our previous job. My gut told me, even though on paper it looked to be a simple, easy job, that it seemed too easy. For once I ignored my instincts and went alone. "

He silently takes in what I am saying and gives me time to regroup. He doesn't push or ask questions I know he has. He is giving me what I need, control.

"The guy was easy enough to find, which in hindsight, should have been my first red flag. I watched him for a few days and learned his pattern and habits. He stuck to the outskirts of Vegas in the seedy rundown bars where no one pays attention. I decided the time was right to bring him in. I parked around the back of the bar and fluffed myself up a little."

I can see his body tense and his jaw grind. He knows he's not going to like what comes next as his body language is screaming, he hasn't liked anything so far.

"I managed to draw his attention quickly, again another red flag, we flirted and did shots. I thought he was intoxicated enough that I could get him out back and subdue him easily. The second we slipped out the back door he attacked me"

Reign can't hold himself back any longer. He drags me into his arms and I go willingly. Wrapped in his embrace, I feel I can continue. Reign gives me strength while not making me feel weak at the same time.

"He choked me a few times and roughed me up. The worst was what he planned to do. He was going to rape me. I could see it in his eyes. Pure evil reflected back at me." I shiver when I remember the look on his face.

Reign tightens his hold on me and buries his face in my hair. Fighting hard to compose himself.

"Did he... Did he rape you?" his voice is so low as he struggles to ask.

"No, he didn't go all the way"

"All the way? Fuck Raven, I need you to explain that, as my mind is running wild and I'm hanging by a thread."

"He touched me but before he could do more, he was stopped."

"Was stopped? Raven, who was the skip you were chasing?"

This is the part I didn't want to discuss. Causing issues between chapters is not something I want to do. He needs to know the Vegas club had my back when I needed them.

"The Vegas chapter was also chasing him, they got there in time to stop him from doing anything more. They helped me. I asked Maddog not to say anything but he wasn't happy about it so we agreed if someone asked, he wouldn't lie."

"Raven, I understand that Maddog had your back as we found you through them so we knew they were involved. I am more than thankful to Maddog for being in the right place. But Raven, you haven't answered my question, who was the skip?"

He is not going to let this go. I'm scared to tell him who it was. Not because I am scared of Reign. Never will I fear Reign, he has a darkness in him but he doesn't use that darkness again women and children. He protects and cherishes them.

"Tyler Cain Jeffreys"

The atmosphere in the room becomes stifling. The sheer amount of rage vibrating from Reign now is powerful. He is battling with his emotions. I huddle in closer to him, holding that if he can feel me, it will calm him.

"Raven, are you telling me that serial rapist, sadistic son of bitch touched you?" he spits out.

"Yes" I answer

"Never again. Never fucking again is evil like that going to touch you."

He lifts my chin so I am looking directly into his face. His eyes swimming with so much passion and love. I have to blink a few times to be sure what I am seeing. Love, Reign loves me.

"You are mine. Not pushing you precious, we will take this at your pace but know this, you are mine. My ol lady, my heart and mine to protect. I am going to kill that son of a bitch, do society a favor."

I take a second to digest what he's said. I never once dreamed that Reign would have the same feelings as me. After everything that has happened, can I let another man in? Except this isn't just any man. This is Reign. I have known him for so many years, I know his character.

Deciding to be brave and take my control back, I move onto my knees in front of him on the bed and lean myself into him. Pressing my lips to his. The lips I have dreamed of kissing and feeling on my body.

He wraps his arms around me, holding me to him as he meets my kiss with his own. Both of us pour our feelings into the kiss. His tongue swipes across my lips, begging for entry to my mouth and I am more than happy to let him.

He pulls his mouth away before we can go any further.

"Are you sure you want this? Once I am inside you, there is no going back" he warns

A warm, delightful shiver passes through me at his words. Like hell do I want to go back. This is everything to me.

"I want this, make me yours Reign," I beg

On a growl, he pounces and I am on my back with him on top of me.

"Gave you an out, you didn't take it. No going back now Raven. You are mine"

With that, he takes my mouth again, his hands roaming all over me. He breaks the kiss and leans up so he can pull his t-shirt off in the sexy move men seem to do, revealing his beautiful torso which could be carved from stone. I can't stop my fingers from reaching out and running them along his abs. Bumps appear where my fingers have trailed showing he is just as affected as me. This gives me a thrill.

He pulls me up so he can pull off the sleep shirt he placed on me earlier, baring myself to him. I know when he spots the now fading bruises as his jaw clenches. I cup his face with my hands and pull his face up so he is now looking at me.

"Just you and me here. In our bed, like this, he doesn't exist. Do not let him take this from me, from us" I beg him

"So, fucking strong and so fucking sexy. Raven, you are beautiful, inside, and out," he says on a breath as I reach for his jeans. Unbuckling his belt and my fingers clumsy struggle with the buttons on his jeans.

He steps off the bed, leaving me laid out for him. He quickly unbuttons his jeans and within a blink of an eye, he's back with me naked. His mouth finds mine in a scorching kiss. He nibbles at my lips, moving to cover my face in small kisses and nips, working his way down my jaw, my neck and onto my breasts.

He kisses the faint finger bruises left and before I can say anything or get lost in my head, he takes my nipple into his mouth and lightly bites. A gasp leaves me as my body arches into his touch as the small bites shoot straight to my clit, making it pulse with need. My hand comes up and threads through his hair, holding his head to me. I scrape my nails across his scalp, causing a groan from him and he doubles his effort switching from one breast to the next, until I am a panting mess.

"More, Reign I need more" I beg him

He chuckles in response and lifts his head to gaze into my eyes, with a wicked grin on his face.

"Your wish is my command, my queen," Jesus fuck, could he get any sexy.

He kisses my breasts one last time before he trails a blazing path down my stomach until is between my legs, I look down at him. With one last sexy smirk, he goes to town on me like a starved man.

His tongue licks me from top to bottom before he nips my clit then sucks into his mouth. My back arches off the bed as pleasure like I have never felt before bolts through me like lightning. He is a man on a mission and I can feel my orgasm building and building to a high I have never felt before.

I feel his fingers at my entrance and my hands instantly shoot out, grabbing the sheet to ground me. The feeling of them sliding into me and then he curls them up to hit that magic spot. That is, it, game over, I peak and come harder than I ever have in my life. I scream his name so loud; my voice becomes hoarse.

He slowly slid his fingers in and out of me, prolonging my high, until I am a pile of mush on the bed. Then pulls them from me and slowly cleans his fingers with his mouth. That should not be as sexy as it is. Just the one crude gesture has me all hot and tingly again, remembering what those fingers just did to me.

"Oh, I am not done with you yet my queen"

I am loving the new name he has for me. The thought of being his queen and meaning that much to him, has shivers of pleasure heightening my arousal. He leans over me, bracing his arms on either side of my head as he cradles me, I feel the head of his cock pushing between my lips as inch by inch he impales me on his cock. The burn from the stretch is delicious and I feel so full.

"Fuck, Jesus Christ baby. I can't drag this out, it feels too good. Like coming home." he pants in my ear before kissing the side of my head as he starts to move. He doesn't hold back and I'm coming on a scream faster than I can blink.

"Give me one more, my queen, that's it, milk my cock. Claim me back"

It is all I need for another orgasm to rip through me and I feel him come with me. My name leaves him in part animalistic growl and a groan of pure pleasure. He drops down next to me, pulling me into him and holding me tight.

"That was everything," he says as sleep drags us both under with happy smiles on our faces.

SEVEN - REIGN

RAVEN HAS been in my bed now for the last week. I have worshipped every inch of her body and consumed her as much as she consumes me. She is now my queen. Proudly wearing my property of cut and getting more to be a little like herself every day.

It was a hard day when we sat down with Tyres and told him what happened, plus how much she was struggling with Banjo's death and the guilt she feels about not being there for him from the start.

She is now getting therapy to help her overcome this, with the full support of myself, her brother, and the whole club. We are all here for her, for anything she needs.

Now is the time to reach out to Maddog. The Vegas chapter had her back when we couldn't. But what Tyler Cain Jeffreys did cannot be allowed to go unpunished. He needs to pay our version of justice for what he has done to Raven and all those other women.

They deserve to sleep peacefully at night, knowing he is not breathing the same air as them. Or breathing any air at all. He needs to go to ground and I want to be the one who causes him the pain he has inflicted on others.

Tyres is with me in the office as Raven is his sister so he deserves to be included in this. Suede and Malice are also present. We are doing this as a club, a family.

"Yes" Maddog answers after a few rings

"Maddog, its Reign"

"She told you then?" he asks straight away

"She did. I want to thank you for having her back when she needed it and we couldn't be there. But he can't be allowed to get away with this. Justice needs to be served, Royal Bastards style"

"Brother, we will always be there if needed. Women are to be cherished. Knew you would be asking so kept up with the case and where our friend Tyler is. He made bail as his father is friends with the judge. He is now back in your neck of the woods. Got a friend who is trailing him and his movements. He can be picked up and delivered to you?" he offers.

Maddog is always thinking ahead. The brother knew we would want justice for Raven. The woman has met anyone who doesn't love her instantly. She just attracts people with her light and goodness. Even being the badass bounty hunter that she is, people are just drawn to her.

"I would very much like that Maddog. You have our marker."

"No marker needed but appreciated. I will arrange delivery and will let you know when the package will be delivered. Have fun with it" he finishes in a dark chuckle.

"Appreciated brother"

We finish the call and I look at Malice. With a nod, he leaves to get our shed ready. Out in the back of the compound we have a soundproof shed we use for our wet work. Makes cleanup easier. We have Elvis for that as he is the club's cleaner and an expert in what he does.

Elvis runs the club's crime scene cleaning business. This is great for two reasons; one it brings in a boatload of money for us and gives us genuine reasons to have access to everything we need for cleaning crime scenes and getting rid of bodies we don't want any finding out about.

"I want in on this Prez. I want to make him bleed for what he did to my sister," Tyres seething says.

"You will do, brother. Would never take that right away from you. I might be her ol man now but you are still her brother and would want to protect her."

"Thanks, Prez, let me know when he's here. I am going to find Debs"

"Claim her brother, good woman, right there. They don't come around too often." I warn

"Just friends Prez. She is too good for the likes of me. My darkness would swallow her light"

It breaks me to think my brother feels like he is not worthy of the love of a good woman. We all are worthy and deserve love. Even the darkest of us deserve some light in our lives.

"Does that mean I am not good enough for Raven?" I ask

He looks shocked by my question.

"Fuck Prez, you are the best thing to happen to Rave, with you I know she will be safe and cared for and you would kill for her."

"So, does Debs not deserve the same? If you are too dark for debs then what the fuck am I?"

I can see the cogs in his mind start to work and think over what I have said. Hopefully, it will sink in. All the brothers deserve goodness in their lives. It is what makes the bad times worth going through so we can enjoy the good.

"I'll think about it," he says as he leaves the room.

Suede and I remain locked in my office. Both quietly thinking over the last week or so in our minds. I can't seem to get what Raven said out of my mind. The skip was too easy, the information was too spot on and detailed than the normal tips they receive.

"It doesn't feel right brother," I say out loud finally

"What doesn't"

"Raven said it was too easy. The skip, information was passed to them about where he would be, it was too detailed and too spot on. She said her instincts threw up a load of red flags but she ignored them."

"You think she was set up?" he asks confused

"It has been playing on my mind but saying it all out loud has confirmed it. But yes, I think it could be possible she was set up. I am going to get Cyber to look into the tip more."

"Good idea, if there is anything to find then Cyber will find it"

Nodding, I send Cyber a message and he confirms he will make it a priority. Now we just need to wait.

"I can feel it in the air Suede, trouble is coming"

It only takes Maddog's friend two days to deliver our package and it is chilling in the shed waiting for us. We are in no rush; he can hang out there for a while.

After he has relaxed for a while, we make our way to the shed. Malice and Country are fired up for this. Country loves to get bloody in creative ways. He looks harmless in his cowboy hat and boots, but the man is lethal.

"How are you hanging there Tyler?" I ask as we enter the shed, causing a few sniggers.

Hanging from the rafters in the middle of the shed by his wrists is Tyler. He has been stripped down to his underwear. Country has the heating set up perfectly so he can make it like an oven one minute and an ice box the next. He will keep switching from one extreme to the other, playing with his prey.

"Go to hell" Tyler spits

"That is where you are going," I warn him

"Now do you understand why you are here Tyler?" I ask

With no answer, Country hits him with the cattle prod, causing him to shout in pain.

"Pussy pissed himself, definitely not a man. Now when Prez asks you a question, you fucking answer him?" Country barks at him.

"She enjoyed it," he says

Yeah, he knows why he is here.

"Like fuck she did?" Tyres growls, looking at me.

CLAIRE SHAW

I give him the nod and take a seat to watch the show.

Tyres jumps straight in and starts using Tyler like a punching bag, careful not to cause too much damage. We want him to suffer. Once he's had enough, Tyres makes his way to the metal bench we have where we store all our toys. He picks up his favorite knife.

He then makes a series of small cuts all over Tyler's torso. Not deep enough to cause damage but just enough to hurt like a bitch. To make it extra painful he rubs salt into the cuts. Tyler is screaming at this point so much his voice is hoarse.

Getting up I place my hand on Tyres shoulder and he relaxes, stepping away. He moves to the corner where we have a sink and shower for us to clean up.

"You touched my woman. You will pay for that" I want just before I plough my fist into him with the knuckle dusters I had slipped on.

I continue to tenderize him as his head drops forward. In my efforts, I almost miss his whispered words, almost.

"What the fuck did you just say?" I demand

"You have no idea what is coming. Raven is just the start of it." he chuckles as blood drips down him.

"What is coming?" Suede steps us and asks.

"He wants Raven and what he wants, he gets"

"Who wants Raven?" growls Tyres

"You can't stop him. Vengeance is coming" he warns as he starts to shake and foam at the mouth.

"Fuck" I groan as the fucker dies.

"What in the James Bond shit was that?" Firefly asks

"Suicide pill. He lasted long enough to pass on the message then took himself out with poison." Country informs us.

"Who the fuck is Vengeance and why are they coming for Raven?" Malice wonders

"Brothers we need to plan, a war is coming. No one is getting their hands on my queen"

Whoever Vengeance is, they have picked on the wrong club. War is coming and we will be ready. Raven is my soul and there is nothing I won't do to protect her.

THE END...... FOR NOW!

CLAIRE SHAW

REIGN: ROYAL BASTARDS MC

DEDICATION

I am absolutely thrilled and excited to be part of the Royal Bastards world. It has been such an honor. I hope you enjoyed the start of Reign and Raven's story. Yes, it was short and sweet but trust me, this is just the start of their journey and that of the Memphis boys.

Raven and Reign will continue in my Christmas book and all will be revealed about Vengeance. Please bear with me while their story unfolds, I promise it will be worth it.

If you have loved Reign, please check out my other books. I love hearing from readers so please, please leave a review.

Firstly, I wanted to thank Crimson for letting me join the ranks of some of my idols and the amazing authors who are part of the Royal Bastard MC universe. I have loved every second of it and can't wait for more.

CLAIRE SHAW

Thank you to my girl Maria Lazarou, for keeping me on track, supporting me no matter what and just being the most amazing friend, a girl could ask for.

To Elizabeth N Harris and Jules Ford…. What can I say, you ladies rock! A huge thank you for checking on me, making sure I was writing and also letting me know it's okay to have bad days. You ladies are true rock stars and I am honored to call you friends.

To all the authors in the Royal Bastards MC universe, you have all made me feel so welcome and been so supportive with my many questions. I am in awe of each and every one of you. Your talents are amazing.

To my poor long-suffering Hubby, Mr. Shaw. Thank you for never letting me give up even when I want to. For bringing me drinks and snacks while I was in my writing cave, lightening my load so I could concentrate on writing, and being my muse and cheerleader. You can have your wife back now…. Until the next book.

And last but never least…. To you, my readers. Thank you for your support, your love, and the love you show my boys is heartwarming and uplifting when I have needed it the most. I hope to never let you down!

I will be back soon with more badass MC alpha males,

Until then…
Love Claire xx

BOOKS BY THE AUTHOR

SONS OF HAVOC - TEXAS CHAPTER
Joker
Carrie's Strength
Tank
A Havoc Holiday
Wire
Wrench

SONS OF HAVOC - PHOENIX CHAPTER
Bishop – Coming Soon

ROAD WRECKERS MC
Chaos – Claire Shaw
Mayhem – Ruby Carter
Psycho – Ellie R Hunter
Riot – Amy Davies

WICKED NIGHTS SERIES
Wicked Lies - Coming soon

ROYAL BASTARDS MC - MEMPHIS CHAPTER
Reign

CLAIRE SHAW

Reign's Queen - Coming Christmas

ABOUT THE AUTHOR

Claire is a Yorkshire lass born and bred. She lives there with her husband, two fur babies, and a large crazy extended family.
Claire is also a huge country music fan and has a bit of an eclectic taste.

Claire has been involved with the indie community for many years now, attending signings, but she also is a PA for authors.

Those authors encouraged Claire to put her ideas and life experiences on paper.
Believing reading is an escape from the pressures of real life, Claire is an avid reader and loves the joy it brings to people.

CLAIRE SHAW

SOCIAL LINKS

Facebook
https://www.facebook.com/Claire-Shaw-Author-113232580058299/

Facebook Group
https://www.facebook.com/groups/662963237528957/

Goodreads
https://www.goodreads.com/author/show/17201274.Claire_Shaw

Website
www.claireshaw.net

CLAIRE SHAW